# FOLLOWING THE

# WHAT IS A HUMAN?

ISBN 9798851347788

Hi friends!

My name is **Ollieolipolipolis**, but my Earth friends call me **Ollie** because Ollieolipolipolis is a little tricky for the human mouth to say. Once upon a time, in a land far far away, I lived on an interesting planet called Oliptario, which orbits the star Rigil Kentaurus. Life was fun and adventurous. My favorite thing to do was research the history and biology of our planet. Oliptario has been around for 1 billion years, which is pretty young for a planet. Since Oliptario is so young, I ran out of things to study, so I decided to come to Earth, which has been around for 4.5 billion years!

Since I'm a researcher and historian, and not an astronaut, I miscalculated some important math. At the beginning of Earth year 2023, I crash landed in the backyard of some humans. Humans are a strange species. Their skin isn't even green, if you can believe it! These humans were very kind. They nursed me back to health, taught me how to speak like an earthling, and invited me to follow them on their adventures so I could learn more about Earth.

This is my personal log of our exploration, insights and planetary history. Join us on our fun adventures as we learn more about the Earth, its landscapes and lifeforms.

**Dear Parents,**

I'm so excited to explore your planet. Thanks for trusting me to learn about history and adventure with your children. My goal is for us to learn **together** and have fun in our family units. I miss my family so much, so thanks for letting me become a part of your family while I visit Earth. My research has been broken into 4 sections. I thought this was a good idea since earth months are broken up into 4 weeks. This will help us learn a little bit each week, so we don't get too overwhelmed. History and research can be a bit daunting! At the end of each section is a suggested family activity. Not only does this help us apply history to our lives, but it helps us bond and create fun memories. Some pages have spaces for what humans have come to call, **"scrapbooking,"** so you can also document your adventures. Most supplies should easily be found around your home, but I'll list them here, so you can be prepared. There will be options for staying at home as well as going out, but the final week will always be focused on going on a family field trip.

Let's have some fun!

Love, Ollie

**Supplies:**

**1.** Small pictures of each member of your family. (See pages 5 and 6 to gage sizes)
**2.** Family memories.
**3.** Pictures of your ancestors (to look at, and/or some copies to add to the book).
**4.** A picture of your family on the field trip.

# WEEK 1

# DESIGNATIONS & PERSONAL HISTORY

# WHAT IS A HUMAN: DESIGNATIONS

Humans have different designations. On my planet, we are all just Oliptarians (you can just call us 'aliens' if you want. I'm fine with that). We are born fully developed, 4 arms and all. When I was two days old, I could already read in three languages! Earthlings don't work that way though. When humans are first born, they don't really do anything. I'm serious! They just kind of lie there and cry a lot. I haven't been around very many of these 'Babies,' but they really just eat, sleep, scream, and vacate their bowels (my humans call this 'Going to the Bathroom'). Babies aren't very good at surviving on their own like young Oliptarians, so they must grow and become strong over time in order to navigate Earth. Since the life cycle of a human seems to be broken into different stages, let's go over the individual designations now, using my adopted human family as an example. They seem to have most of the designations we'll be looking at.

**These are my humans:**

**Adult:** Legally this is someone over the age of 18 years old, but really, it's just someone that does a thing some adults call, "adulting." That usually means they have a job and pay bills. My adults are called Mom, Dad, and Max. Max is such an adult that he lives on the other side of the world. It's so far away that it is tomorrow there! Adults can also be very old too. Weird!

### DESIGNATION: DAD

**Height:** 6' 2"
**Age:** 45 years
**Abilities:** Apparently, he writes stuff for other people to read, but it isn't science. Weird!

### DESIGNATION: MOM

**Height:** 5' 6"
**Age:** 43 years
**Abilities:** Teaches children about science, math, and literature. She is pretty amazing, and my favorite!

### DESIGNATION: MAX

**Height:** 6' 2"
**Age:** 19
**Abilities:** Teaches people about something called 'Religion' in a place called 'New Zealand.'

**Teenagers or adolescents:** humans count the years they are alive, or the number of times the earth has gone around the sun since they were born. Any age that ends in the word, "teen" is considered a teenager. Some people say, "ugh, teenagers are the worst," but I don't think that's true. The teenagers I know are super cool. They work really hard to learn new things. Sometimes they work so hard that they get real tired and their faces look a little grumpy. When that happens, I give them something yummy to eat and tell them how cool they are, and then they feel better. I have one teenager in my adoptive family, her name is Elese. She is six-TEEN years old. She likes to sew and play the guitar and she's really good at both those things.

**DESIGNATION: ELESE**

**Height:** 5' 7"
**Age:** 16
**Abilities:** Plays a musical instrument called a 'Guitar.' Also makes clothing using a sewing machine.

**DESIGNATION: SAM**

**Height:** 5' 2"
**Age:** 12
**Abilities:** Builds constructs with building blocks called 'Legos.' Also plays a sport called 'Baseball.'

**DESIGNATION: OLIVIA**

**Height:** 4' 6"
**Age:** 10
**Abilities:** Draws, reads, rides her bicycle, and laughs a lot. She is also very vocal. Never silent.

**DESIGNATION: MEGAN**

**Height:** 4' 2"
**Age:** 7
**Abilities:** Wiggles a lot. Never really sits still. Also loves science and experimenting, like me!

**Children:** Children are too young to be teenagers or adults. They have gone around the sun 1-12 times. My adopted family of humans has four designated children. Sam is 12, he likes Legos and Dungeons and Dragons. Olivia is 10. She likes to sing and dance and play with friends. Megan is 7. Megan is wiggly. She reminds me of the wiggily Wompam from my planet. They summersault wherever they go, just like Megan. Dashel is 5. He likes He-man, which is a fictional character. Dash likes He-Man a lot.

**DESIGNATION: DASHEL**

**Height:** 3' 6"
**Age:** 5
**Abilities:** Loves He-Man. Runs a lot. He's fun to play with and is always learning. Dash is my Friend.

**Babies:** My humans don't have babies, but they all used to be babies. Historically, everyone must be a baby. No one starts out as an adult. The adult women are pretty cool and they grow the babies in their bodies.

# THE IMPORTANCE OF PERSONAL HISTORY

Every person has a history. It's their 'Personal History.' I've learned that personal history is every bit as important as world history because it's the story of each of us individually. For example, Human Dad lived in 3 different states when he was a child and teenager. He used to work in television but now he is an author. Mom lived in the same house until she met Dad and got married. She liked to be in plays when she was a teenager. Sometimes history repeats itself because she started being in plays again. Elese used to only be able to sew a straight line and play one chord on the guitar, but now she can make Prom dresses and play lots of songs. Sam used to only play with Legos, but now he plays baseball too. Personal history matters!

# YOUR PERSONAL HISTORY

You personal history, and the history of your family, is incredibly important! I'm learning that as I live with humans. Imagine if no one ever recorded their own hisotry. So much fun knowledge would be lost. Let's have some fun! On this page I want you to write a bit about yourself. What are a few things you like to do? What is your favorite place to visit? Share your personal history so you won't forget these details!

My favorite food is_____

My favorite activity is_____

My favorite place to visit is_____

My happiest memory was when_____
_____
_____
_____
_____

08

Now it's your turn to classify your family. What is your designation? Put photos of your family members under the proper designations. Make sure to include pictures of yourself!

**MY FAMILY**

**CHILD**

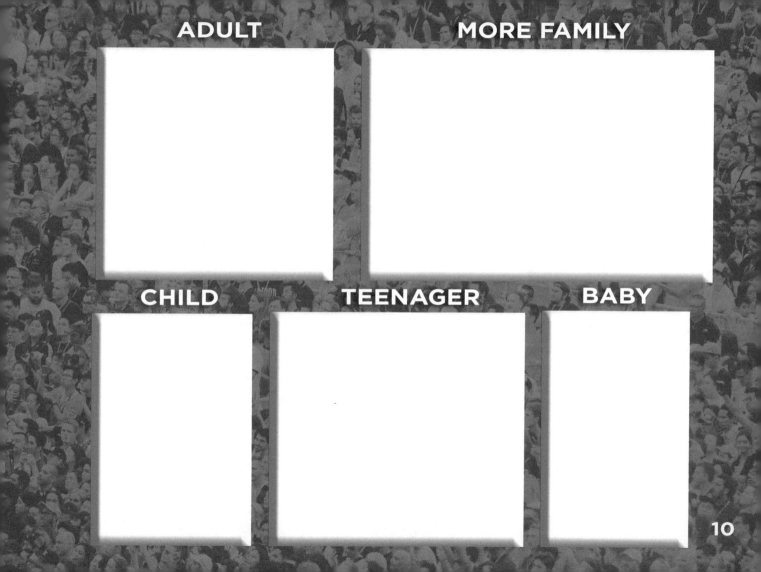

ADULT

MORE FAMILY

CHILD

TEENAGER

BABY

10

# WEEK 2

# HUMAN HISTORY

I'm learning that all life on Planet Earth is made up of tiny pieces called 'cells.' They are so small you need a microscope to even see them. These cells perform specific jobs in the body. I got to see what a giant cell would look like at the museum. Can you believe that you have between 30 and 40 trillion cells in your body right now?

13

In order for me to learn more about Humans, my humans have taken me to a museum to learn the history of humans. This museum had lots of cool information. Over time, humans have changed quite a bit. This museum talked about humans from all over the world. We could make 100 books from everything we found at this museum, but, for this book, we are going to focus on diversity (how people are different) and the history of humans in general. Did you know that humans are actually called 'Homo sapiens?' Homo sapien means 'Wise Man' in an old language called Latin. According to current theories and evidence, Homo sapiens evolved about 200,000 years ago on the continent of Africa. That's a long time ago!

# Neanderthal and Early Humans

Humans have an interesting history. Did you know there were actually more than one subspecies of human? A subspecies is formed when a part of an animal population lives off by itself and evolves unique traits over time. For example, I have antenna and four arms because my species evolved that way. Humans had several subspecies like Neanderthal, who had bigger foreheads and stronger muscles. Homo Floresiensis is a more recent subspecies that was actually much shorter than modern humans. They were only about my height, or three feet tall. That's pretty short, especially if you look at humans today. The reason we know about these subspecies is because of scientific studies, fossilized bones, and even genetic analysis. I learned that scientists are discovering new fossils all the time!

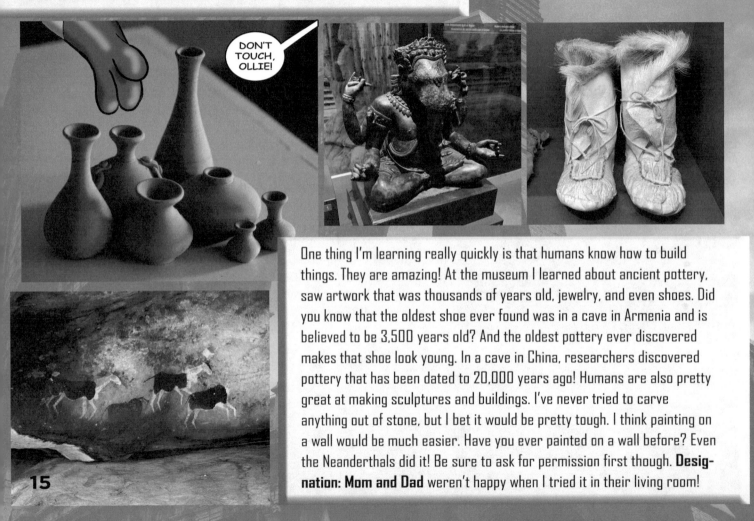

DON'T TOUCH, OLLIE!

One thing I'm learning really quickly is that humans know how to build things. They are amazing! At the museum I learned about ancient pottery, saw artwork that was thousands of years old, jewelry, and even shoes. Did you know that the oldest shoe ever found was in a cave in Armenia and is believed to be 3,500 years old? And the oldest pottery ever discovered makes that shoe look young. In a cave in China, researchers discovered pottery that has been dated to 20,000 years ago! Humans are also pretty great at making sculptures and buildings. I've never tried to carve anything out of stone, but I bet it would be pretty tough. I think painting on a wall would be much easier. Have you ever painted on a wall before? Even the Neanderthals did it! Be sure to ask for permission first though. **Designation: Mom and Dad** weren't happy when I tried it in their living room!

15

WE CAN DO IT, DESIGNATION: CHILDREN! KEEP WORKING!

While my humans were learning about tools and art, the **Designation: Children** found a fun puzzle game that showed how people who study prehistory, or 'Archeologists,' put broken pottery back together. It's harder than it looks, but we got it done. Sam and I were the best at it! The most important thing to look for when putting pottery puzzles together is to pay attention to the pattern painted on the outside, then it's easy!

DID YOU KNOW:
Pottery is a very ancient human invention. It dates back tens of thousands of years. The way people make pottery has remained pretty much the same during all that time. You can put thin layers one on top of the other, or spin the pottery on a wheel.

16

Historians learn a lot about what they are studying by doing research. That means studying books and asking questions.

Research your humans!

Look into your family history. If your grown ups don't know about where your family came from, ask **Designation: Grandparent.** They've been around for a while and know lots of stuff. Look at old family photos, a genealogy app, or visit a relative.

Old family photos can be lots of fun to look at. These are some of Mom's grandparents. They liked to write poetry. Dad's grandpa was really good at making things. He made this plate for Dad when he was a little boy. What fun things did you find out? Answer the questions on the next page.

What countries are your ancestors from? _____

What did your grandparents do for work? _____

Does your family name mean anything? (My humans' name means Hay-man in German. They think their ancestors must have been Germans who worked with hay)

_____

Put some pictures of your historical humans in the spaces on this page.

Historical Human!

Historical Hu

WEEK 3

# BUILDING CIVILIZATION

# HISTORY: BUILDINGS AND CIVILIZATIONS

El Castillo in Yucatan, Mexico

The Pyramid of Giza in Egypt

We've already learned that humans have been around a long time, but one of the coolest things about them is that a lot of the stuff they've built over those thousands of years is still around today. Humans have built some amazing buildings and monuments all over the world. Early humans started to live together in large groups once they figured out how to farm and raise animals. Because of farming, food became more plentiful, and suddenly humans were able to concentrate on things outside of hunting and finding their next meal; things like art and architecture. They established what are called 'Civilizations' about 10 to 15 thousand years ago. These civilizations built pyramids like the ones in Egypt and Central America, as well as giant walls in China, and mountaintop cities in Peru. I knew humans were smart, but it's pretty impressive that the oldest building in the world is 10,000 years old, maybe even older!

The Great Wall of China.
Can you see me on the wall?

Machu Pichu, Aguas Calientes, Peru

Petra, Wadi Musa, Jordan

Rome, Italy

Taj Mahal, Agra, India

DID YOU KNOW?
When I arrived on Earth I thought human buildings were pretty impressive. As I've studied ancient (that's another word for 'really old') structures, I've discovered that even 10,000 years ago, humans knew how to build. Many of the oldest buildings were made of stone blocks. Some were carved right into the rock itself, while in Turkey there is an entire city built underground!

22

# RESEARCHER'S LOG: FOOD

One thing I've learned about human civilization is that their food is just as important as their buildings! Humans love food, and why wouldn't they? On my planet, Oliptario, we generally eat nothing but protein paste with vegetable extract. Imagine eating your tooth-paste and you're pretty close to what it's like. On Earth though, food is amazing! I love all of it! Pizza, steak, grilled vegetables, tacos, eggs, carrots, salad, chicken, hamburgers, everything! Oh, and ice cream! Do you like ice cream? Ice cream is the best! Green and colorful vegetables are amazing. I've learned to cook a few recipes with my humans. Cooking is like a science experiment. It's fun!

23

DID YOU KNOW?
Eating meat is believed to have contributed to early human brain development and growth in size.

# JOIN THE FUN

## ACTIVITY TIME!

What is your favorite food? Have you ever tried to make it yourself? Well, now is your chance! Sit down with your designated adult (Mom, Dad, Grandma, etc.) and talk about your favorite food and how to make it. Follow the recipe and make it with your adult's help. Afterward, write down how it went below. Was the food good? What went wrong? What went right? Tell me everything!

_____
_____
_____
_____
_____
_____
_____

DID YOU KNOW?
Pizza, Turkish kebabs, hamburgers, and falafel from the Middle East are the most popular foods in the world. Which is your favorite?

WEEK 4

# BIOLOGICAL DIVERSITY

# RESEARCHER'S LOG: BIOLOGICAL DIVERSITY

Just like humans have different age designations, they have other differences as well. Sometimes humans use the word, "diversity," to describe these differences. Diverse means 'variety,' or having many different variations. The more differences you have, the more fun things become. On my planet, Oliptario, all the living beings look pretty much the same as I do: green skin, three fingers on each hand, and two antenna. Most of the plants are pretty similar to each other too. It's a beautiful place, but not very exciting, if you ask me.

Here on Earth though, I discoverd so many different types of people, plants and animals. It's so amazing! I've been to planets where they only had one plant. That was really boring. Earth has lots of different plants. They all look so interesting. People aren't all the same, and it makes things way more fun.

Different types of dogs

**DID YOU KNOW?**
There are 360 different dog breeds recognized by the International Canine Federation!

Plant diversity

Human diversity

**WE'RE A PRETTY DIVERSE GROUP**

# RESEARCHER'S LOG: HUMAN DIVERSITY

Just like plants and animals, humans are very diverse too. Humans have different heights, different shoe sizes, and different skin colors. The reasons for these differences have to do with something called 'Genetics,' which is the study of heredity and genes, or in other words, the physical qualities we all get from our parents. Skin color is a very interesting one for me, since everyone on my planet is green. Humans have different skin colors because of melanin, which is a natural pigment found in almost all organisms (I have melanin too, it's just green!). If your body produces more melanin, your hair and skin will be darker. That trait is then passed from parents to children. Many humans refer to these skin color differences as meaning someone is of a different 'Race,' even though all humans are the same 'race.' In fact, modern science considers race to be a social construct, not a biological one.

## JOIN THE FUN

Diversity isn't scary, it's just different. The more differences I've observed on planet Earth, the more I've learned that even though humans are all unique, they are all just...well...humans. They are simply beings with interests, friends, families, talents, insecurities, confidence, fears, dreams, and most of all, just humans who want to give and receive love. We all have unique DNA, so there are a lot of fun differences to notice. Do you want to learn more about diversity? Find your grown-ups and let's get started. A big part of science is observation. For this activity, we are going to focus on observating.

1. Look at images online (or in a book) of different humans. How many differences can you find?

2. Walk around your neighborhood. How many different types of plants can you count?

3. Do you have pets? How are your pets different from humans? How are they the same?

4. Find a cultural center in your city that focuses on a different culture than yours. Go there!

# DISCUSSION TIME!

Now that you've done some observating, it's time to talk to your grwon-ups about what you noticed, particularly about the different people you saw. Ask each other the questions below and discuss.

1. What color are your eyes?
2. Does anyone in your family have the same color?
3. Did you notice any really cool looking eyes while you observed others?
4. What color is your skin?
5. Does anyone in your family have the same color?
6. Did you notice any beautiful people that may have skin that looks different than yours?
7. Do any members of your family have freckles? Some of my humans do, but not all of them.
8. Did you notice anyone whose body moved differently than yours?
9. Were some humans you observed different sizes and shapes?
10. Write something that you noticed about the babies, children, teenagers, and adults that you observed.
11. How are you the same as the people you saw?
12. How are you different?

30

# FAMILY FIELD TRIP!

Each month I'm going to invite your family to go on one big adventure to study what we've talked about and learned over the month. So that means it's time for a family field trip! Here are some fun things that I've done during my time on this planet, but if you have an idea that works better for your family, then go for it!

Go to a park or the mall and 'people-watch.' It's fun to see how people look and act differently when they are playing or having fun.

Visit an older relative and ask about their personal history.

Visit a museum near you.   Go to a local cultural event.

Try new foods that humans who are different than you like to eat.

# WHAT DID YOU LEARN?

Paste or tape field trip photos below!

Well, fellow explorers and scientists, that's it for this month. I hope you learned a lot about humans! I know I did. I'm just beginning my journey here on Planet Earth, and I am so excited to follow my humans on many more great adventures. Remember, every month you can come with me and learn new things if you want to. I'll be going to amazing places like the Redwood Forest, learning about airplanes and aviation, visiting ocean ecosystems, and even going back in time to see how humans used to live. Join me for some fun and learning. I hope to see you there!

JOIN US FOR THE FURTHER ADVENTURES OF OLLIE THE ALIEN AND HIS HUMANS!

SUBSCRIBE HERE:

www.followingthehumans.com

# FOLLOWING THE HUMANS

## BOOK 002

# TO THE
# REDWOODS

# FOLLOWING THE HUMANS
## BOOK 002
# TO THE
# REDWOODS

WOW! THESE TREES ARE GIANT!

Hi friends!

Ollie here! I hope you're ready for adventure, because this month we are going to a place that is so big, you're going to feel like an ant! I'm so excited!

Did you know that every 4th grader in the United States can get a free National Parks Pass? **Designation: Olivia** got one this year, so my human family wanted to put it to good use. But first, they had to tell me what a 'National Park' is.

Earth is a beautiful place with lots of diversity. In order to protect and help that diversity grow, nations (countries) turn these extra special places into parks. Then they hire 'Park Rangers' and other helpers to keep things beautiful and make sure the animals that live there are protected and wild.

Olivia wanted to go to the Redwood Forest. It is a National Park in California. This park spreads across 172 square miles and also includes some state parks. This park interested her because it has the tallest tree on earth! How tall do you think it is? HINT: the answer is hidden on this page!

The tallest redwood is 380 feet tall!

Another reason Olivia thought it would be pretty cool to go to the Redwood Forest is because New Zealand, where her brother, **Designation: Max**, currently lives, also has Redwood trees. And guess where they got their Redwoods? California!

So, if you're ready, let's head to the Redwoods! If you've never been before, don't worry, we're going to show off the trees, the environment, and learn a bunch of stuff along the way. Let's start now with some trivia about the Redwood Forest!

## REDWOOD FACTS

1. A Redwood's leaves can actually get water from fog.
2. Redwood bark can be up to a foot thick and is resistant to fire and rot.
3. A Redwood can live for over 3,000 years!
4. The Redwood Forest takes up over 48,000 acres growing in 75 destinct groves.
5. Some Redwood fossils date back to the Jurassic age of the dinosaurs!
6. The roots of Reedwoods touch each other, allowing them to stabilize each other during powerful storms.
7. Only 5% of the original Redwood Forest remains after a century of logging.

REDWOOD FOREST IN ORANGE

That's the entire state of California right there! The Redwood Forest is really massive!

# WEEK 1

# VISITOR CENTER LEARNING

While exploring the Visitor Center, we found a a stump with antlers growing out of it! Turns out an elk died a long time ago in the crook of the tree and the tree grew around it. Crazy!

After a really long drive, (we were in the car for two days!) we finally got to the Redwood forest. Our first stop was the Visitor Center. Have you ever been to a Visitors Center? They usually have maps to the places you're visiting, nearby trails and areas to explore, helpers to tell you the coolest things to see, and the little humans favorite part: souvenirs. Olivia chose the Junior Ranger hat as her souvenir.

If you ever visit a National Park Visitor Center, you can ask them how you can become a Junior Ranger. You even get a cool pin to wear. I got one, and I wear it proudly.

Olivia had a burning question about the Redwood Forest, so while at the Visitors Center, she asked the Park Ranger her question.

Park Rangers are amazing helpers. Not only do they know everything about the park, but they also know how to keep people safe. They are the police officers of the park. Some of them even go to college and study the same things as police officers! **Designation: Max** wants to be a Park Ranger when he returns from New Zealand.

So what question did Olivia want to have answered so badly? Turn the page if you want to know the question, and the answer.

**DID YOU KNOW?**
National Park Service Rangers all wear 'flat hats' that first became official parts of their uniforms in 1920. The hats help protect Rangers from hot sun and cold rain but also represents the passion they have for nature.

Olivia's burning question was, "When was the last fire in the Redwood Forest?"

Do you see what I did there? Earthlings would call that "punny" because I used a pun. Puns are things that have a double meaning. Her **burning** question was about **fire**. Get it?!? That's funny, right???

Anyway, that amazing Park Ranger was so smart because she knew the answer. She said they don't know when the last fire was because it was before people started keeping records, so that must have been a long time ago. Because of the fire damage left behind though, they are able to estimate that the last fire in the Redwood Forest was over 250 years ago! She even told us where to go to see some of the burned out trees.

They looked so cool and we even got to climb inside them. Afterward I wanted to know more, so I did some research. Guess what!? Redwood trees are fire resistant. They have lots of tannin and thick bark which makes it really hard to burn! The inside of the tree will burn, but not the outside, and even then, the tree will still survive even though the middle got burned away. It has a superpower against fire!

This Visitors Center had a trail right nearby. It was very beautiful and we had so much fun exploring. We found a bridge and started throwing leaves into the water and watching them all slowly float away. It's really fun being in a new place because even though we are used to seeing plants and animals at home, the plants and animals here all look a little different. We even got to see a gang of elk!

You may not be close to the Redwood Forest, but getting out into nature is still pretty easy, even if you live in a big city. Go for a walk around your neighborhood, or even just sit in your yard, and pay attention to the nature that surrounds you. Are there things that you're so used to seeing that you forgot how beautiful they were?

What animals did you see? _____

What part of the experience did you like most? _____

What plants did you see? _____

Did you see any insects? What kinds? _____

How many different types of trees did you see? _____

What type of environment are you in? Desert? Forest? Urban? Swamp? _____

45

Post some pictures of the beauty you discovered. You could even find a flower and press it inside the pages of this book.

# WEEK 2

# WHAT IS A FOREST?

Some of you who live in more urban areas might not be familiar with forests, while those of you who live in rural areas might even have a forest in your backyard. Either way, it's important to understand what a forest is, what differnt types of forests look like, and how they affect the environments around them. On my home planet we have a giant forest with pink trees that turn blue in the fall. I haven't found any forests like that here on Earth, but I have been surprised by how many different types of forests grow here. So, what is a forest exactly? You'd think that would be an easy question to answer, but it actually isn't! A forest is understood to be an area that has lots and lots of trees, but that only depends on where the forest is. Some scientists think the trees have to be a certain height to be considered a forest, while others say it depends on the animals that live there, or the location of the largest group of trees. See? Not as easy to answer as we thought. Science can get a bit complicated sometimes.

A deer in a Coniferous Forest

A Russian forest in December

LOOK! I'M BALANCING ON AN ABIOTIC ROCK WITH MEGAN AND OLIVIA!

**DID YOU KNOW?**
One of the important aspects of a forest are things that are 'abiotic.' Abiotic means anything that isn't alive. You would think that would mean they aren't important to a forest, but they are! Rocks, rain, sunlight, soil, and climate are all abiotic, and without those things, the forest wouldn't be able to survive.

One thing is for sure: the dominant plants in a forest are trees. The types of trees can be completely different one forest to the next because of things like soil type, moisture, climate, and sunlight. We'll examine different types of forests in a minute, but for now, let's look at the basic things needed for an area to be considered a forest. First, you need trees, obviously. Then you need other smaller plants, animals, and insects. What I've discovered by studying forests, is that forests are all about life; plant lfe, animal life, all sorts of life! There are even entire cities inside forests that are still conidered part of the forest because they have trees, and other plant life (shrubs, bushes, flowers and grass), while also having lots of animals (squirells, birds, dogs, cats, and people). Even the cars and buildings are considered part of the forest because, just like rain and sunlight, they affect all the plant and animal life in the area!

I know we are visiting the Redwood Forest, but I think it's important for us to realize that not all forests have Redwood trees, so let's learn about different types of forests.

51

Tropical Rainforests: These ones are really neat. I got to visit one with my human family on the island of Maui. It was so beautiful and peaceful. Some rainforests have monkeys and other crazy wildlife. Deignation: Mom and Dad visited a rainforest in Costa Rica where a monkey tried to steal their lunch. So, if you're ever in a rainforest, keep your sandwich close. These forests are really green because they get lots of RAIN! Rainforests have what they call 'closed canopies.' That means the trees grow together and create a sort of ceiling over your head. Rainforests don't have Redwood trees, they have Rubber, Ramon, Kapot, Brazil Nut, and lots of other types of trees.

Evergreen Forests: These forests have evergreen trees. If you're good at watching for clues, you might guess that evergreen trees stay green forever. Well, you'd be right. During a holiday called Christmas, my humans put an evergreen tree inside their house! It smells really nice. There are lots of different types of evergreen trees, but some that you've probably heard of before are Pine Trees and Furr Trees.

Quaking Aspen Forest: Pretty soon I will get to visit one of these. Every summer my humans go to a cabin in a Quaking Aspen Forest. These trees are tall, but not as tall as Redwoods. They are white with green leaves, but they aren't evergreen. Quaking Aspen are deciduous, that means they lose their leaves in the fall.

Forests fit under three categories: Temperate, boreal, and Tropical.
1. A Temperate forest is a forest that has different seasons. Sometimes it is hot and sometimes it is cold. These usually have deciduous trees.
2. A Boreal forest usually has deciduous trees too, but they also have Evergreen trees.
3. A Tropical forest is a forest that has rain all year long. It never has a dry season.

## JOIN THE FUN

Based off what you've learned, match the images of the forests on the right with the names and descriptions on the left.

TEMPERATE FOREST _____

BOREAL FOREST _____

TROPICAL FOREST _____

A forest with 6 to 8 months of freezing temperatures, mostly evergreen trees but some deciduous too.
**What type of forest am I?** _____

A forest with all four seasons, (warm to cold) made up mostly of deciduous trees.
**What type of forest am I?** _____

A forest with consistent high temperatures and lots of rain all year long.
**What type of forest am I?** _____

# ACTIVITY: MATCH THE TREES

Look at the trees below and write down what type of forest you would find them in; Evergreen, Rainforest, Boreal, or Temperate.

WE ARE IN A TEMPERATE FOREST RIGHT NOW!

_____

_____

_____

_____

_____

_____

# WEEK 3

# BIG TREES & HISTORIES

# REDWOOD HISTORY

Redwoods have been around for 240 million years! That's a long time. The Redwood Forest in California is about 20 million years old. Humans started encroaching on the forest about 150 years ago. Since then, 95% of the forest has been cut down. Currently, the Redwood Forest is protected, with new growth returning to areas that were cut down.

**DID YOU KNOW?**
Redwoods can grow 1 to 2 feet per year until they reach 200 to 300 feet tall. They live for thousands of years, and some of their growth rings are so small they can only be seen under a microscope. After decades of logging, it is now illegal to cut down a Giant Redwood tree.

When building the Redwood Highway, which currently runs 230 miles from San Fransisco to Grants Pass, Oregon, logging camps sprung up where lumberjacks cut down trees along the future roadway. The original route passed through over 2 million acres of Redwood forest.

Contruction on the highway began in 1911. Before that only a dirt trail called Mail Ridge Road existed that was primarily traveled by riders on horseback (I want to ride a horse!). The road wasn't completed until 1920, 9 years later, and even then the highway had spots that were difficult to drive through in rainy conditions. Today, Highway 101 is a much better road, and what used to take four days can now be driven in about four hours!

58

# THE BIG TREE

You would think that all the trees in the Redwood Forest would be BIG, and they are, but there is one that is bigger than most of the others. They decided to name it **'Big Tree.'** I would have called it, **'Gargantua Major-Tree Rex,'** but I guess 'Big Tree' is fine. The Big Tree has a circumference (how big around it is) of 74 and a half feet, it's 285 feet tall, with a diameter (how far across it is) of almost 24 feet.

Now you might be wondering how old the Big Tree is if it's so giant. I know I was! Well, no one knows for sure. Redwoods grow more complex as they get older, so evidence suggests Big Tree could be one of the oldest trees in the entire forest! Let's look at some of the evidence!

Sometimes really old Redwoods like Big Tree will have a second tree growing out of the original trunk. These are called 'Reiterated Trunks.' Big Tree has several!

Epiphytes are another way to know Big Tree is really old. Epiphytes are plants that grow on other plants. Ferns and huckleberries grow 200 feet up on Big Tree where soil and water collect!

## JOIN THE FUN

Wow! That tree was so big! My planet has trees, but nothing like these. Have you ever seen a tree that big? Even though the trees around your home may not be gigantic, they are still beautiful and helpful to your community. Did you know that trees provide oxygen for humans and humans help trees by breathing out carbon dioxide? This is called a symbiotic relationship. That means that we help the trees and they help us. To show appreciation for the trees near you, look around your yard, or neighborhood, to find the biggest tree in your area. Be sure to bring your grown-up and a camera. Then, give it a hug. How many of you did it take to hug the tree? Don't forget to take a picture, print it out, and put it on the next page so you can remember that you hugged a tree.

THIS IS A BIG TREE.

Our local tree.

How many people it took to hug the tree!

# WEEK 4

# EXPLORING THE REDWOODS

While we were at the Redwood Forest, we did a lot of exploring. Do you know what an explorer is? I guess I'm an explorer of sorts. An explorer is someone who travels to a new place and learns about it. As we explored the forest we did all sorts of things to help us better understand our surroundings. We walked across giant logs, we looked at plants, and we even counted tree rings.

THIS TREE IS GROWING FROM THE STUMP OF ANOTHER TREE!

DID YOU KNOW?
Redwood trees can be found in different places around the world, but the reason there aren't large forests of Rewoods anywhere but California is because it is the one place on Earth where the climate and elevation combine to create the right conditions for the forest to thrive. It's always wet here, even during droughts.

65

First, we kept our eyes out for bears. We didn't want to bump into one of those. Then we touched the tree bark. It felt soft and spongy, not hard and rough like the trees we were familiar with. I noticed that the forest smelt fresh, like earth and dirt. I liked hearing the birds chirping. The children, and Dad, liked to explore by climbing on trees and rocks. Mom preferred walking along the uneven ground. It was very bumpy because of dirt, rocks, and redwood needles. She also stood by to make sure everyone was safe and well fed. She had lots of snacks. Some tasted salty and others tasted sweet.

It's important for explorers to use all their senses so they can really get to know a place or culture. Normally we think about 5 senses; sight, smell, taste, touch, and smell. We used all theses senses while exploring the Redwoods (Remember? We looked for bears, we touched the trees, we smelled the forest air, we heard the birds, and we tasted Mom's snacks). But did you notice that we used two other senses too? Yep! There are actually 7 senses, but we usually just talk about 5. The lesser-known senses are a little bit harder to say, so that's probably why we don't talk about them much.

So what are these other two senses that nobody talks about? They are called the **vestibular** and **proprioceptive** senses. Try and say both of those words real quick. It's hard, huh? It took me a bit of practice to say them right with my alien tongue.

The vestibular sense helps us with balance. My humans used this sense while walking on the uneven ground. Without this sense, people wouldn't be able to jump or run and would fall down all the time. The proprioceptive sense helps us know where all our body parts are even when we aren't looking at them. Go ahead and close your eyes real quick. Now move your arms. Do you still know where your arms are even though you can't see them? That's the proprioceptive sense at work! Dad and the kids used their proprioceptive sense when they were climbing because they couldn't always see their hands and feet as they climbed. I use this sense a lot since I have 4 arms and 2 legs. That's a lot to keep track of. I don't know how you humans do it with only two arms!

**Explore your home and yard using all 7 of your senses.**

TASTE

SIGHT

HEARING

TOUCH

PROPRIOCEPTIVE

SMELL

VESTIBULAR

# Come back here and write down what things you discovered!

What did you see and how did it look? (colors, textures etc) _____
_____
_____
_____

What did you touch and how did it feel?_____
_____
_____
_____

What does your house or yard smell like? Was anyone baking cookies or barbequing?_____
_____

Is your house noisy? Mine is! What did you hear?_____

How did you use your balance to explore?_____
_____
_____

# FAMILY FIELD TRIP!

For this month's family field trip, go to a local forest or large grove of trees and have a family picnic. Depending on where you live, there may not be a forest near you. In that case, find any natural area away from cities or towns where you can enjoy the wild world. It may even be a desert! It doesn't matter. Go there and have a picinic together. While enjoying nature, pay attention to what you see, hear, and experience. Are the trees and plants different here than they are around your home? What is the same? What is unique? Do you see any wildlife like squirrels or lizards? What birds do you see?

BONUS ACTIVITY: Play Hide-N-Seek as a family! Who had the best hiding place?

THIS IS A NICE SPOT!

My humans and me on a picnic in a nearby forest.

# WHAT DID YOU LEARN?

Paste or tape field trip photos below!

Well, I hope you enjoyed this month's adventure! Going to the Redwood Forest was a real thrill, and I learned so much about the natural world here on Earth. I had no idea trees could grow that big, and live that long. Plus, being able to climb around was super fun! Have you ever been to the Redwood Forest before? If you have, go to my website, **www.followingthehumans.com** and share your photos. I love learning about other families and their adventures. And if you want to see me visit a specific place to learn more about it, tell me on the website! You never know, I might just show up and ask you a whole bunch of questions about where you live. I'm having so much fun on Earth. This really is a great place to live and explore, and when we can do that with our friends and family, the people we love most, it is even better! See you next month!

SUBSCRIBE AND JOIN US FOR THE FURTHER ADVENTURES OF OLLIE THE ALIEN AND HIS HUMANS!

NEXT MONTH:

*The Humans Learn to Fly!!!!!!!*

**www.followingthehumans.com**

74

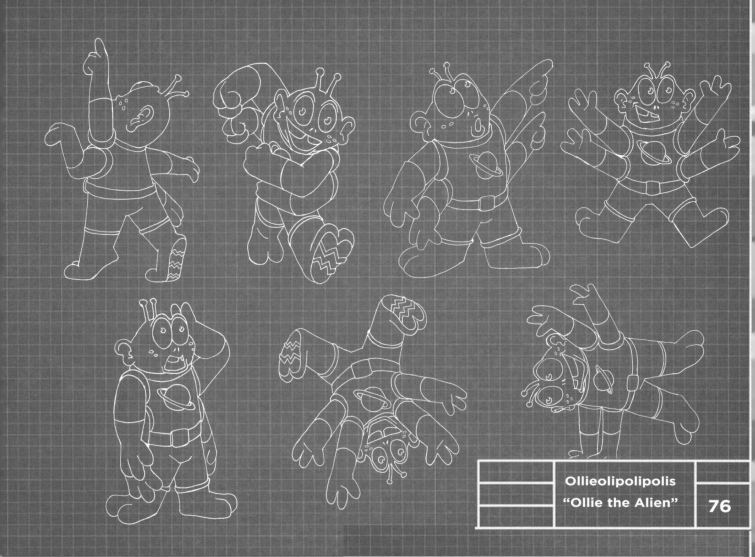

# More books for kids and families from the Following Humans Team!

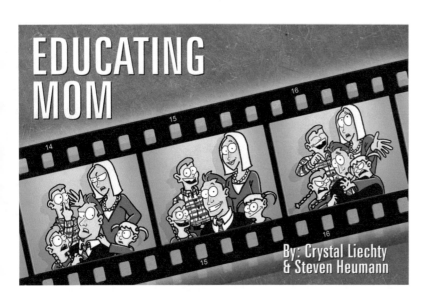

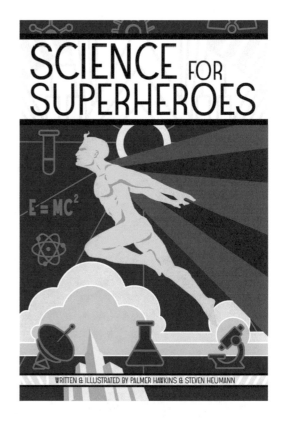

# Fun, adventure, and laughs for the whole family!

Made in the USA
Thornton, CO
03/05/24 16:26:56

31cd9687-7e8b-4e7c-b6ee-3fe52270cf95R01